Sally and Max are visiting the museum.

The museum has an exhibition all about dinosaurs, and Sally and Max love dinosaurs.

There are levers to pull,

buttons to press,

bones to dig,

This Walker book belongs to:

_____

_____

For Ben and Emily x
Thank you for all of your expert
dinosaur advice

First published in Great Britain 2019 by Walker Books Ltd
87 Vauxhall Walk, London SE11 5HJ

10 9 8 7 6 5 4 3 2 1

© 2019 Sara Acton

The right of Sara Acton to be identified as the author and illustrator of this
work has been asserted by her in accordance with the Copyright, Designs and
Patents Act 1988

This book has been typeset in Kosmik PlainOne

Printed in China

British Library Cataloguing in Publication Data: a catalogue record for this
book is available from the British Library

ISBN 978-1-4063-8795-7

www.walker.co.uk

Dinosaur Day Out

Sara Acton

WALKER BOOKS

AND SUBSIDIARIES

LONDON • BOSTON • SYDNEY • AUCKLAND

facts to read

and great, big ...

DINOSAURS
THIS
WAY
→

dinosaurs.

But today the dinosaur exhibition is closed.

So Dad buys a book all about dinosaurs,

and they head into the city.

In the city there are large, leafy gardens,

with pathways to explore

and trees to climb.

"Did you know," said Dad, having a rest on a bench,
"that the diplodocus was the longest-known dinosaur

and loved to snack on leaves?"

"And the pterodactyl," said Dad,
tucking into a tuna sandwich,

"was a large winged lizard that
hung out in trees and ate fish."

Sally and Max had a drink at the fountain,

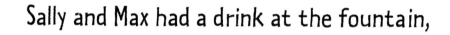

and Dad bought a
ticket for the train ride.

"Did you know," said Dad, climbing aboard, "that the stegosaurus had spectacular bony plates running down its back and was as big as a bus?"

"And the tyrannosaurus rex," said Dad, choosing
a double scoop of mint chocolate chip ice cream,

"was a ferocious meat-eater, with huge
teeth and tiny little arms."

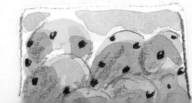

The sun shone down and the sea shimmered in the harbour.

"Did you know," said Dad, shooing a seagull away from his
ice cream, "that the spinosaurus was the biggest carnivorous
dinosaur of all and ate fish, including sharks?"

"And the sarcosuchus," said Dad, peering into a pond dotted with lily pads and lotus flowers, "was an enormous crocodile, with massive jaws and a powerful bite."

The sun started to dip and descend and the sky became a warm glow.

"Time to go home," said Dad, "for a bite to eat."

"Did you know," said Dad, as they
hurried back through the park,
"that some dinosaurs hunted in packs?"

"While others," said Dad, as they reached
the train station, "were masters of disguise."

They scraped through the gate,

scrambled down the steps

and caught the train ...

PULL
IN CASE
OF
EMERGENCY

just in time.

"I'm sorry we didn't see any dinosaurs," said Dad. "Maybe they needed a day off."

Sally and Max peered out of the window and smiled.